Puppies for Rosie

BY MICHÈLE DUFRESNE

CONTENTS

Pioneer Valley Educational Press, Inc.

Puppies for Rosie

"I wish we had
a puppy," said Rosie.

"Oh, no," said Bella.
"We do *not*
want a puppy!"

"I wish we had
two puppies,"
said Rosie.
"I love puppies.
Puppies are fun.
Puppies are very cute!"

A little puppy peeked
out of a box.
"Hello!
My name is Daisy.
I will be your puppy,"
said Daisy.

Another puppy peeked
out of the box.
"Hello!
My name is Jack.
I will be your puppy,
too!" said Jack.

Rosie was so happy!
"Look! *Two* cute
little puppies,"
she said. "They are
just what I wished for."

Jack and Daisy
found a slipper.
"I've got it!" said Jack.

"No, *I've* got it,"
said Daisy.
They played tug-of-war
with the slipper.

Jack and Daisy
found a newspaper
on the floor.

"I've got it!" said Jack.

"No, *I've* got it,"
said Daisy.

They played tug-of-war
with the newspaper.

Rosie walked around
the house looking
at the mess.
"Oh, dear," she said.
"Oh, dear!"

Jack and Daisy
made puddles.
They made puddles
in the kitchen.

They made puddles
in the living room.

Rosie walked around
the house looking
at the puddles.
"Oh, dear," she said.
"Oh, dear!"

The puppies made
a puddle on Rosie's pillow.

"This is disgusting!"
said Rosie.
"Jack and Daisy are little
but they are *not* cute."

"I *told* you we did not want a puppy," said Bella.

Puppies for Rosie: The Play

Rosie

I wish we had a puppy.

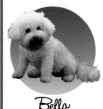
Bella

Oh, no. We do *not* want a puppy!

Rosie

I wish we had *two* puppies. I love puppies. Puppies are fun. Puppies are very cute!

Narrator

Two little puppies peeked out of a box.

Daisy

Hello! My name is Daisy. I will be your puppy.

Jack

Hello! My name is Jack. I will be your puppy, too!

Rosie

Look! *Two* cute little puppies. Just what I wished for.

Narrator: Jack and Daisy found a slipper.

Jack: I've got it!

Daisy: No, *I've* got it!

Narrator: Jack and Daisy found a newspaper on the floor.

Jack: I've got it!

Daisy: No, *I've* got it.

Narrator

Jack and Daisy made puddles.

Rosie

Oh, dear. Oh, dear! This is disgusting! Jack and Daisy are little but they are *not* cute.

Bella

I *told* you we did not want a puppy.

Puppies are baby dogs.
Some puppies will
not get big.
Here is a small puppy.
He will stay small.

Here is a small puppy.
He will not stay small.
He will grow and grow.

Puppies like to sleep.

They like to eat.

They like to play, too.